WALTER DEAN MYERS

The Black Pearl & The Ghost

OR

One Mystery After Another

ILLUSTRATED BY

ROBERT QUACKENBUSH

DR. ARAMY
—
Great
Detective

MR. DIBBLE
—
Ghost
Catcher

The Viking Press
New York

For Piet, who likes mysteries and ghost stories   R.Q.

CONTENTS

First Edition
Copyright © Walter Dean Myers, 1980
Illustrations Copyright © Robert Quackenbush, 1980
All rights reserved
First published in 1980 by The Viking Press
625 Madison Avenue, New York, N.Y. 10022
Published simultaneously in Canada by
Penguin Books Canada Limited
Printed in U.S.A.
1 2 3 4 5 84 83 82 81 80

Library of Congress Cataloging in Publication Data
Myers, Walter Dean. The black pearl and the ghost.
Summary: Two stories: one featuring a great
detective in search of a missing pearl, one with a
famous ghost chaser tracking down a mischievous ghost.
1. Detective and mystery stories, American.
[1. Mystery and detective stories] I. Myers, Walter Dean.
Mr. Dibble and the ghost of Bleek Manor. 1980.
II. Quackenbush, Robert M.   III. Title.
IV. Title: One mystery after another.
PZ7.M992B 1980   [Fic]   79-20268   ISBN 0-670-17284-7

The Black Pearl of Kowloon

"It's gone! It's gone!" Mr. Uppley ran to the attic. He banged on Dr. Aramy's door. "It's gone! It's gone!" he cried.

Dr. Aramy had been asleep. He opened his eyes one at a time. He put on his fuzzy slippers. Then he opened the door. "What is gone, Mr. Uppley?"

"The Black Pearl of Kowloon, sir."

"The one they were to give to the Queen?"

"The very one, Dr. Aramy. I just received the call from the Kowloon Hotel."

Dr. Aramy was a great detective. Mr. Uppley was his faithful friend. Together they set out for Kowloon. They rode their two-seater to the river. They took the ferry to Kowloon. Soon they were at the hotel.

The manager was quite upset. "Thank heaven you are here," he said. "I have locked the doors to the hotel. No one has left or come in."

"Is this where the pearl was kept?" Dr. Aramy held his magnifying glass near the display case. It was empty. He looked along the walls. And on the floor. And under the corner of the rug. No pearl. Finally he discovered a clue. It was a shoe. In the shoe was a foot. It was attached to a large person.

"Who are all these people?" Dr. Aramy asked.

"This is Billy, the bellboy. This is Donald, the desk clerk. This is Charles, the chef. This is Garibaldi, the guard. This is Thomas, the tourist, and this is Sister Norbert, the nun."

"They were all here when the pearl was stolen?" Dr. Aramy asked.

"Yes."

"Only they and no one else?"

"That is correct."

"Then they are all suspects! Now tell me about the display case, please." Dr. Aramy sat down in a large, stuffed chair. He adjusted the brim of his bowler. And took a small pinch of snuff.

"Well," began the manager, "the pearl was in the display case, which was covered by a velvet cloth. Suddenly there was a cry of fire."

"Zut! Fire, did you say?" Dr. Aramy jumped to his feet.

"Yes, but there is more."

"There is, my good man, no need for more. Who called out 'fire!'?"

"The desk clerk." ·

"He, then, is the thief." Dr. Aramy hit the desk with his cane. "He called out 'fire!' There was, of course, no fire. He just wanted everyone to run about. So he could steal the pearl. Arrest him at once!"

"But there was a fire," said the manager.

"There was?"

"And when the call was made, he was at his desk."

"He was? Pity. Do go on."

"There was a cry of fire! Smoke was coming from the kitchen . . ."

"From the kitchen, you say?"

"Yes, but there is more."

"There is no need for more, dear fellow. We have our man. Arrest the chef!"

"The chef?"

"Of course. How clear it all is! He set the fire in the kitchen. Knowing, of course, that the alarm would be given. When it was, there was confusion. Except for the man who set the fire. Then he crept out and stole the pearl. It's probably under his hat now!" Dr. Aramy knocked the chef's hat off. There was no pearl under the hat.

"But it was he who put *out* the fire," the manager said, picking up the hat.

"It was?"

"Yes," the manager said.

"Pity. Go on with the story."

"Then the lights went out . . ."

"The lights?" asked Mr. Uppley.

"Yes," the manager said. "And when they came on again, I looked under the black velvet cloth. Which was, by the way, wet."

"Zut! Did you say that it was wet?"

"Well, just the corner," said the manager. "But there is more."

"Fool! How could you be so blind?" Dr. Aramy said. "We have found the thief!"

"Well done!" said Mr. Uppley.

"Well done!" they all said.

"Who is it?" asked the manager.

"It has to be the guard, of course. When everyone was looking the other way, he went into the kitchen and set the fire. Then he turned out the lights. He stole the pearl. Then went back to his post. But it is a well-known fact that thieves have sweaty hands. He was standing near the case and wiped his sweaty hands on the velvet cloth."

So they searched the guard. They searched his turban and boots, his pockets, and even his beard. But they found no pearl.

"He doesn't have it," said the manager.

"He doesn't?" said Dr. Aramy. "Pity. But let me ask a few questions." Dr. Aramy pulled at his left ear. "Was everyone seated when the lights went on?"

"Yes," the manager said.

"Just as they are now?"

"Yes," said the manager.

"So—the pearl was stolen. And then the thief ran back to his chair. From where did the sounds come?"

"The sounds?" asked the manager. "What sounds?"

"The sounds of footsteps made by the thief."

"We heard nothing," the chef said.

"I did not ask you, my good fellow. You've caused enough trouble already."

"We heard nothing," said the manager.

"Surely the case cannot be this clear!" said Dr. Aramy.

"Why, I do believe he's solved the case," said Mr. Uppley, waking from a short nap.

"The thief set a fire in the kitchen, ran and turned off the lights, ran to the display case and stole the pearl, wiped his sweaty hands on the cloth. But!!! And mind you well the 'but.' No steps were heard across the floor. And why not? Ah, it is quite simple. The thief does not wear shoes!"

"No shoes?" said Mr. Uppley. "Indeed!"

"Most of us," said Dr. Aramy, "wear shoes. It is the habit of well-mannered people. But one of us, in habit, has her feet hidden! To conceal the fact that she wears no shoes."

"But surely you can't mean—?" Mr. Uppley gasped.

"But I do mean it," said Dr. Aramy. With that he leaped toward the nun. He grasped the bottom of her habit and, after turning his eyes away, he lifted it to her knees.

"Oh!" and "Dear me!" the nun cried.

"But she *is* wearing shoes!" the manager said.

"She is?" said Dr. Aramy.

"Saints preserve me!" said the nun. And fainted dead away.

"Dear me," said Mr. Uppley. "The thief is still afoot. And, it would seem, the foot is shod."

"Did I tell you that we found a clue?" the manager asked as he fanned the nun.

16

"A clue?" said Mr. Uppley.

"We found a false moustache. It was in front of the display case."

"Tell me if it is red or black," said Dr. Aramy, standing on a chair.

"It is red," said the manager.

"Then we must be going," said Dr. Aramy, "after, of course, we collect our fee. For this case is solved. The crime went like this. The thief set a fire in the kitchen. Then came through the door yelling 'fire!' He turned off the lights. Then he tippytoed over to the pearl. But—he dropped his false moustache. The one clue that gave him away. Who here wears a moustache?"

"Thomas, the tourist," said Mr. Uppley. "But his is black."

"And as false as the red one," said Dr. Aramy. Then, faster than a bee's blink, Dr. Aramy grabbed Thomas's moustache and yanked it with all his strength.

"*Ooooooweeeee!* You fool," said Thomas. "This moustache is real!"

"It is?"

"It is."

"Not false?"

"Not false."

"Pity. But then it is not a clue."

"There is another clue," said the desk clerk.

"What is it?"

"It is an order for a blueberry tart."

"Zut! Why was this not brought to me before?" Dr. Aramy turned very red. "Was the tart to be delivered to a room?"

"Why, yes," said the desk clerk.

"And who was to deliver it?"

"Billy, the bellboy."

"Kind sir! Kind sir!" the bellboy said.

"Beg not for mercy, wicked lad, for justice falls hard upon the bad."

"But, sir," said the bellboy, "when the call of fire came I was sitting. The nun was so scared that she fainted, as you see she easily does. She landed upon my lap and stayed there. I could not move. I could not have taken the pearl."

"You could not have?"

"I am afraid not."

"You are quite sure."

"Quite, sir."

"Pity."

"A genuine shame," said Mr. Uppley. "We have failed to solve the case."

"A shame? Yes," said Dr. Aramy. "But we have not failed to solve the case."

"And who do you accuse now?" asked the manager.

"Why, you, of course," said Dr. Aramy.

"Oh, how absurd," the manager said.

"Yes, is it not? May I have a cup of tea? And, perhaps, a blueberry tart?"

"But how did he do it?" asked Mr. Uppley.

"Simple," said Dr. Aramy. "First he stole the pearl, then he slipped into the kitchen. He hid the pearl and started the fire. Then he wanted to cause confusion, so he turned out the lights. In the darkness he dropped his false moustache and the order for the blueberry tart in which he had hidden the pearl! Which is why he had to wash his hands and later wipe them on the cloth. The one covering the display case."

Dr. Aramy reached into the tart, pushed about with his finger, then pulled out the Black Pearl of Kowloon.

"Gadzooks!" cried the manager. "I am caught! But you will never take me alive!" With that he ran toward the door. "*Oooff!*" Mr. Uppley grabbed him by the legs and sat upon him until the police arrived.

"Dr. Aramy, what put you on to him?" asked Mr. Uppley as they wheeled back to the ferry.

"Simple," said Dr. Aramy. "The cloth was wet on the left side. I noticed that the manager was left-handed. And put two and two together."

"But the cloth was wet on the right side," said Mr. Uppley. "Not the left."

"Not the left?"

"I am afraid not."

"Pity," said Dr. Aramy. "It would have been such a good clue."

The Ghost of Bleek Manor

A letter came for Mr. Dibble, the famous ghost chaser. "You must come right away," it read, "to see about the ghost of Bleek Manor."

Well, to be sure, Mr. Dibble was tired. He had taken care of two ghosts that very week. One he had chased from an old castle. The other he had found hiding in a cellar. But it was his job, and so off he drove to Bleek Manor.

The door was opened by Lord Bleek himself.

"I am here to see about your ghost," said Mr. Dibble.

"At last," said Lord Bleek. "I have not slept in days."

"Tell me how he bothers you," said Mr. Dibble.

"Well," said Lord Bleek, "every night before I go to bed I check all the doors and put out the lights. Then, in the middle of the night, I hear a strange noise. It sounds like this: Shla-THUMP! Shla-THUMP!"

Mr. Dibble took out his ghost book. He looked up *Shla-THUMP!*

"Oh, yes, of course," he said. "Ghosts often float about in their sleep, you know. When they hit the ceiling or the wall, they go Shla-THUMP! Quite simple. But not to worry. For I know what we must do. We must get a silk cord. One end we will tie to a corner of the bed. The other end we will tie to a silver bell mounted on a hickory post. Then when the ghost begins to float about, he will pull upon the silk cord, which will ring the silver bell, which will wake him up at once!"

"Oh, yes, that is very good," said Lord Bleek. And that very night they tied a silk cord to one end of the bed, then across the bed to the top of a hickory post, where they attached it to a silver bell.

And it seemed to work. To be sure, they still heard some noises during the night. The silver bell rang twice. But no Shla-THUMP! Shla-THUMP! Shla-THUMP! Lord Bleek was very happy.

"I will send you my bill," said Mr. Dibble, putting on his cap.

"But what about the awful screams?" said Lord Bleek.

"Awful screams?" said Mr. Dibble.

"Sometimes," said Lord Bleek, "I hear a scritching and a scratching like something creeping along the floor. And then I hear these awful screams that make my blood run cold."

Mr. Dibble took out his ghost book again. He looked up *Awful Screams*. "Oh, yes, here it is," he said. "Your ghost must pay for the bad he has done. The finger of fate comes to him and scratches on the wall. It shows the ghost the evil he has done and how he will be punished. When the ghost sees that," said Mr. Dibble, "he screams in terror! But not to worry, my good friend. The answer is here in this book. We must find a black cat that has but one ear. We must tie a red ribbon around its neck and put it in the room with the ghost. Have you heard the saying, 'The cat has his tongue'?"

"You mean—"

"Yes," said Mr. Dibble. "It is a well-known fact that a cat will grab a ghost's tongue so he will not be able to scream."

So they found a black cat with only one ear. They put a red ribbon around its neck and put it in the room with the ghost.

That night they heard no scratching sounds. They heard no awful screams. Just the sound of the cat jumping about. Lord Bleek was very happy indeed.

"I will send my bill," said Mr. Dibble.

"But what about the banging shutters?" said Lord Bleek.

"Banging shutters?" said Mr. Dibble.

"Yes," said Lord Bleek. "I keep the shutters closed. But sometimes when I cannot sleep, and turn to the comfort of my books, I hear the shutters banging open."

"Well, dear me," said Mr. Dibble. He took out his ghost book again. "Yes, here we are. *Shutters; Banging.* Some ghosts like to fly about at night. They like to go through the window. When they do, the shutters bang. Simple enough, I suppose. We must take a bowler and put tiny holes in it. We then hang the bowler from the ceiling and put a flashlight behind it. When the ghost wakes and sees the tiny spots of light, he will think that they are stars and fly into the bowler. And, of course, if he cannot get out before morning, we will have him!"

So they got a bowler and put very small holes in it. They placed a flashlight behind it and hung the whole affair from the ceiling. Sure enough, that night there were no banging shutters. Although the bowler was empty in the morning, Lord Bleek shook his head happily. He was quite pleased.

"I will send you my bill," said Mr. Dibble. This time he did not put on his cap.

"But what about the groans that come from the cellar?" asked Lord Bleek.

"The cellar, too?"

"I am afraid so," said Lord Bleek. "I hear them often. As if something were down there, moving about in the musty darkness."

"Oh, well," said Mr. Dibble, who already had his ghost book out. "I am afraid this is rather serious. For if the ghost can sleep peacefully for three nights straight in the cellar of a house, you cannot ever get him to leave!"

"Dear me!" said Lord Bleek.

"But not to worry," said Mr. Dibble. "For he must be able to sleep peacefully. And that we will not allow. We must take chicken fat and smear it upon the top two steps leading to the cellar. The ghost will fall down the stairs onto a slide. The slide will lead to a mattress. Under the mattress there will be springs of all sizes. He will bounce about like a ball and will be only too glad to leave the cellar and, perhaps, the house."

So they put the mattress and the springs of all sizes at the bottom of the stairs. Then they put the slide up to the middle of the stairs. Then they smeared the top two steps with chicken fat.

That night they heard nothing. No groans from the cellar. No banging shutters. No awful screams. And no Shla-THUMP! Shla-THUMP!

"And that," said Mr. Dibble, "is that! Isn't it, Lord Bleek?"

"Oh, that it is," said Lord Bleek, "if one doesn't mind the creaking stairs."

Mr. Dibble did not answer Lord Bleek. Instead he turned quickly to *Stairs; Creaking*, in his ghost book.

"Um-hm!" he said. "Ah-hah!"

"What does it say?" asked Lord Bleek.

"It says, my good man, that ghosts signal other ghosts in the area by making things creak. There are door-creakers, shutter-creakers, floor-creakers, et cetera . . . your ghost is a stair-creaker. If we leave him alone, he will have every ghost in the neighborhood in your house!"

"How dreadful!"

"But we can beat him. When he uses his powers to make the stairs creak, we will use ours to make them stop. We will put a fan at the bottom of the stairs. Over the stairs we will put a large pot of honey and several large pillows. The pillows will muffle the sound of the creaking until the honey gets into the cracks, blown there by the fan, of course."

"How clever!" said Lord Bleek.

So they put a large pot of honey over the stairs, as well as several large pillows. At the bottom of the stairs they placed a large fan. Then they waited until they heard the stairs creaking. Lord Bleek turned on the fan while Mr. Dibble tipped over the honey and pushed the pillows onto the staircase.

They heard no more strange sounds that night. Or the next. Not even one.

"Is there anything else?" asked Mr. Dibble.

"Nothing at all," said Lord Bleek. "You may send me your bill."

Mr. Dibble and Lord Bleek shook hands. And that was the end of the ghost who lived in Bleek Manor.